PIECES

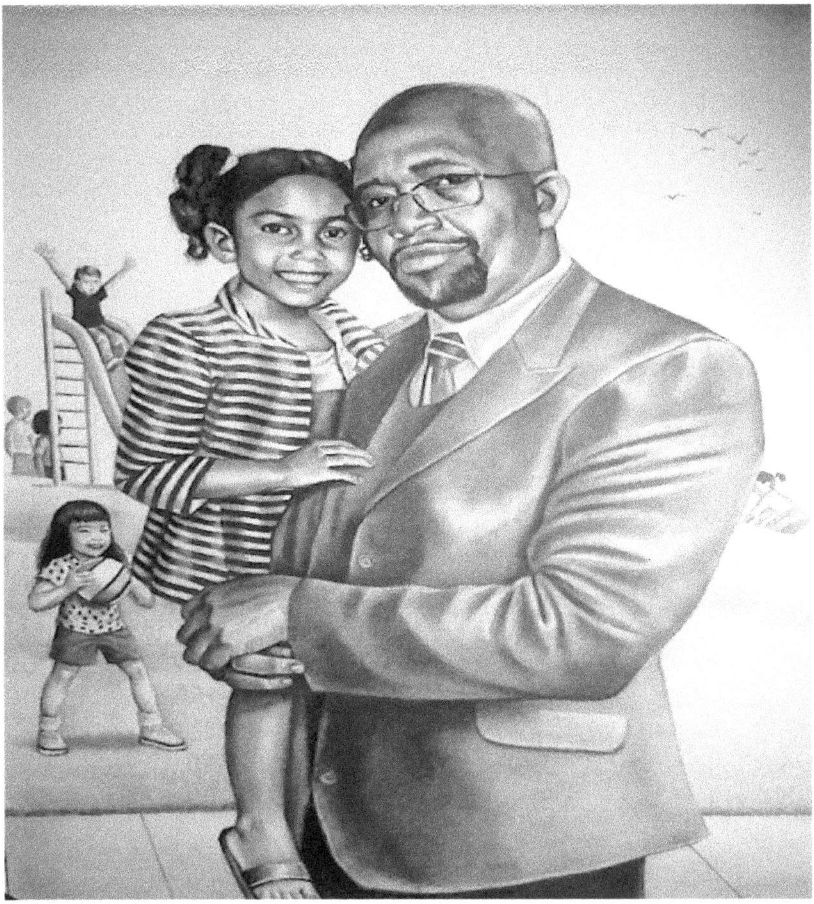

THE BROKEN LIVES OF MANY PEOPLE

CONTENTS

This book is dedicated to families who have experience tragedy due to domestic violence and brokenness due to unresolved situations. This book was based on the life and death of my baby daughter Zaneta Hatch.

ACKNOWLEDGEMENTS

Writing this book was a special experience. It brought back many memories and confirmed the need for a book like this. The many young women who have encountered domestic violence relationships and teens who get involved in drugs and gang violence are the central focus for creating this work.

While writing this book, I was fortunate to have the help and support of some outstanding people; Dr. Gary Hatfield, Mrs. Rita Hatfield and Zaneta former counselor, Theresa Scott who was a ram in a bush after I heard that my daughter had died. She taught me through my distress while driving after the death of my daughter.

I am deeply indebted to Mrs. Rita Hatfield for editing this book. I give thanks to Mr. Curtis E. James for allowing me to use his original artwork, "Granddaddy Baby" on the front cover.

Dr. David A. Hatch

THE MISSING PIECE

The loss of my child was a tragic event

I felt like it tore out my heart

The tears would flow endlessly day in and day out

My whole world was falling apart

Life was so broken

There now was a huge missing piece

I cried out, out to God, "How could this happen?"

It seemed the pain would never cease

I searched the scriptures to find some comfort

I needed relief for my soul

I knew that God loved me and He had the answer

I knew that God wanted me to be whole

I read about peace that passes understanding

I read about peace ruling my heart

I found the Lord of peace will give me peace in every way

God has given me a new start

He opened my eyes and allowed me to see

That the missing *piece* was the missing *peace*

I am no longer bound to a life of pain

Praise God! I can now be free.

PIECES

Chapter One

THE BEGINNING

There was a cool crispness in the air that indicated winter was coming very soon. It was too soon for Keirra because Christmas would be here shortly. Keirra remembered when the Christmas season was a joyful and exciting time. She looked forward to unwrapping all those gifts and anticipated she would soon be seeing all the favorite toys she had dreamed about. Christmas for Kierra was always so wonderful. She seemed to exist in a different world back then. The kind of world little girls dream of: the white house with the red painted door sitting in the middle of an enormous yard with plush green grass and flowers, surrounded by a white picket fence, a little dog named "Spot" lounging in his doghouse, and the family gathered together as they did year after year for the annual "Soul Food Feast". Everyone always seemed so happy and hugs and kisses and smiles were given and welcomed. This was the dream world she lived in as a child. Things seemed to change quickly as she grew older. The dream world she had as a child began to fade. Time no longer seemed to stand still. Keirra was growing up.

Keirra's parents divorced when she was young and she began to struggle with who she should be loyal to, her mother or her father. She did not want to take sides because she loved them both. Divorce is always difficult for children and in Keirra's case, it was extremely difficult. She seemed to have no sense of belonging or purpose and she began to look desperately for something or someone to give her life meaning.

When Keirra was a freshman in high school she had a boyfriend named Quant. He was involved in selling drugs and Keirra became accustomed to this activity and it did not seem wrong or abnormal to her. It was pretty much an everyday way of life. After all, there were so many people she knew who did the same thing. She believed this is just how things were if you needed to make money.

Keirra was in her second period class impatiently waiting for this school day to be over. She was glad to hear the bell ring. The hallway was soon filled with students going from one class to another. Quant met Keirra at her locker. Keirra was excited to see him and said, "Quant, I miss you. We haven't spent much time together lately." Quant replied," I know it baby, but I've been on the grind trying to make it happen. On the real, a brother trying to make some money, ya know, so we can be happy!" As Keirra looked at him with a dreamy look in her eyes, she said, "I hear you, but I still miss you." Quant hesitated for a minute and then he said, "I tell you what. Me and you. Tonight. No interruptions." Keirra said with excitement, "Sounds good to me!" Quant watched Keirra rush down the hallway so she would not be late for class.

Quant headed outside to the building next door for his next class and he was startled by Jody, one of Quant's drug customers. Jody was a very big guy and he was visibly upset with Quant. He spoke in a threatening manner as he told Quant that the drugs he had sold him the night before were no good and he wanted his money back. Quant tried not to let it show but he was afraid of Jody and he quickly told him he did not know the drugs were bad and he would try to get his money back in a few days. Jody yelled at him, "You sold me some bad stuff and I want my money back. Now!" Quant knew this guy was an addict and he was very unstable. Quant said, "It's not my fault, man, just chill out and I will get you your money back but I don't have any money on me right now." Quant told Jody he had to get to class and he would see him in a few days with the money. As he tried to walk away, Jody grabbed him and started hitting him. Quant tried to fight back, but Jody was much bigger and stronger than Quant. Jody relentlessly beat up Quant and left him lying on the sidewalk bleeding and in pain. Quant was found by a teacher and was taken to the hospital.

Before the school day was over, Keirra heard about what happened to Quant and she immediately left school and got a ride to the hospital where Quant had been taken. She was so upset and she wasn't sure what kind of condition he was in. He had been admitted to the hospital so she knew his injuries must be pretty severe. As she entered the room and saw Quant lying on the bed, battered and bruised, she began to cry. She ran to his side but he was barely conscious. Jody had broken three of Quants ribs and his eyes were very swollen. He had cuts on his face where he had been hit so hard.

Eight days later Quant was released from the hospital. It took him a while to recover and he was out of school for a few weeks. Keirra tried to spend time with him while he was recovering but because of school and not having transportation, she was not able to see him much. During this time Keirra had all kinds of thoughts about what happened. She began to question herself about having a boyfriend who was a drug dealer. Surely this was a freak thing and something like this would probably never happen again. She convinced herself that everything would be okay.

After a few months Keirra's relationship with Quant began to fade. He was fully recovered from his injuries and he continued to deal drugs but he was spending less time with her now than ever before. Keirra was always upset about Quant not spending time with her and the time they were together was spent arguing. Finally, their relationship came to an end. This was only the first of a long line of relationships with guys that Keirra had and none of them ever lasted very long.

Chapter 2

TEVIN'S NEW PERSPECTIVE

When Keirra turned sixteen she met a guy named Gary. He was 32 years old and he showed a lot of interest in Keirra. Gary was a good looking man and Keirra really like that he paid attention to her. He being older was attractive to her too. Gary told her he liked her because she was mature for her age and Keirra believed everything he told her. She was hoping this was "the one". Keirra loved it that Gary would always pick her up and take her places. He took her back and forth to school every day. She felt safe and secure with him.

Gary had been married previously and had a son named Tevin, who was 14 years old. Keirra knew about Tevin from the beginning of their relationship and she was not troubled by the fact that Tevin was almost as old as she was. Tevin lived with his mother, Theresa, and his sister, Erika. Gary was not Erika's father. Gary had visitation with Tevin two times a month and also paid child support. Keirra did not really understand what kind of an impact these things would eventually have on her relationship with Gary. After Keirra got out of high school, she and Gary moved in together. Keirra was really looking forward to a great life together with Gary.

Tevin was used to hearing his mom complain about his dad and she blamed him for all of their problems. Tevin had mixed feelings about his dad because of the way his mom talked about him but Tevin also wanted his father in his life. He missed having a dad and wanted to spend more time with him. He was a little confused about his dad's new girlfriend. He did not know what to make of his dad living with such a young woman. This new relationship his dad had just seemed to add to Tevin's frustration about spending time with his dad. He was often torn between the anger he felt because he did not have his dad in the house and the gladness he had when his dad did come around. Sometimes Tevin was angry when Gary came to pick him up. Tevin felt like his dad did not really care because he was not there very much and he hardly ever called him. Tevin had a pretty hopeless outlook on life as he watched his mom have such hard time making money and saw that his dad did not help them very much. It did not take much for Tevin to be drawn into a life of theft and drugs. He had promised his mother that he would not go that direction but he ended up there anyway. He felt like he had nothing to lose.

Tevin met a guy named Julius one day as he was walking home from school. Julius introduced Tevin to the drug trade. He told Tevin he could make a lot of money and it was easy. This was tempting to Tevin especially after seeing his mom struggle so much to buy food and pay bills. Tevin knew he did not want to keep living that way.

Tevin told Julius that he was interested and asked him what he needed to do. Julius told him he would give him some pills to give away for the first couple of weeks so people could try it out and then they would come back for more to buy. "Free samples" is what he said promoted business.

Tevin was excited about his new venture. He started handing out free drugs to a lot of people and sure enough, after a short while, many of those same people came to him to buy more. Tevin could hardly believe how easy this was! When he realized how much money he could make, he decided that was what he was going to do from then on. Tevin got a little greedy along the way and started taking a little more than his share of money. For a couple of weeks in a row when he came to pay Julius he did not have all the money he owed him. Julius was not happy about that and came to the school where he found Tevin and told him to pay up. Tevin was scared and assured him he would have his money the next day. Julius said, "You better have it or you are a dead man! I will meet you right here tomorrow at 12:00 outside the lunch room." Tevin was terrified because he did not have the money and did not know how to get it by the next day.

Tevin went home hoping he would figure out a way to get Julius' money. He knew his mom did not have any money and he did not want to ask his dad because he would have to explain why he needed it and he figured his dad would not have the money anyway. He thought about not going to school the next day but Julius knew where he lived and Tevin was afraid he would come to his house. The next day when Tevin got to school, he started asking other students if they could loan him some money. Most of them said they had no money and some looked at him like he was crazy and told him no.

The closer it got to lunch time the more frightened Tevin got. He was really desperate now and he had an idea. He knew his first period teacher always brought her purse into the classroom and put it under the desk by her chair. He was going to wait for the opportunity to snatch her purse when she wasn't looking and see if she had any money in it. Of course she was there all during first period and everyone would see him so he decided to wait until class was over. When it was time to go to his second period class, as everyone was walking out of the room, he kind of lagged behind. The teacher was erasing the board and was not looking. As soon as Tevin had a chance when no one was looking he walked by the teacher's desk and grabbed her purse. He hurried outside and ran behind a building where he searched through the purse looking for money. He found a twenty dollar bill, which was nowhere near the amount he owed Julius. Tevin tucked the money away in his pocket and tossed the purse into the dumpster. Tevin went on to his next two classes, wondering what he was going to do.

When the bell rang for him to go to lunch, Tevin headed for the building farthest away from the lunch room, where he stayed, hiding from Julius. He figured he would stay behind the building for a while and Julius would go away. After about an hour, Tevin came out and walked down the sidewalk in front of the school office. Suddenly Julius came around the corner and Tevin could tell he was furious. Julius shouted at him, "You can't hide from me; I will find you wherever you go!" Julius pulls out a gun and points it a Tevin. Tevin cries, "Julius, please, I got some of your money!" Tevin pulls out the twenty dollars he had stolen from his teacher and hands it to Julius. Julius grabbed the money and said, "Where is the rest of my money?" Tevin begged him, "Give me chance man, I really tried to get your money today. This is all I could come up with. I will pay you back as soon as I can!"   Julius said, "I told you yesterday if you did not have my money today you were a dead man!" Tevin pleaded with Julius, "Come on man, please don't kill me!"

Just about that time the principal, Mr. Matthews, walks out the door of the office and yells at Julius to put the gun down and get away from Tevin. Julius knew Mr. Matthews from years before when he was in school. Julius was surprised to see him and said, " Well, look who's here, been a long time since I saw you." Mr. Matthews finally talked Julius into letting Tevin go and he ran and got behind the principal to get away from Julius. Julius called Tevin a coward and told him he better stay out of his way or he would get hurt.   As Julius walks off down the street, he yells out at Tevin, "This is not over, I will get my money!"

Mr. Matthews immediately calls the police and tells them one of his students had been threatened by someone with a gun. Two police cars show up quickly and he told the police Julius' name and gave them a description of him. Mr. Matthews points them in the direction he had gone. The police drove off quickly looking for Julius. One of the officers stayed behind to talk to Tevin and Mr. Matthews. Tevin lied and told the police that he had borrowed some money from Julius and could not pay him back right away and that was why Julius was so mad at him. The police officer knew there was probably much more to the event than what Tevin was telling him but Tevin stuck to his story. Mr. Matthews also knew that Tevin was involved in something dangerous and illegal but he had no proof. The police found Julius right away and he was carrying a stolen gun. Julius was arrested and taken to jail. The police contacted Tevin's mother and she came to pick him up. Tevin told his mother the same story he had told the police.

Before Tevin's mother got there, he thanked Mr. Matthews for stepping in and stopping Julius. He knew he would probably have been shot and it really scared him. Mr. Matthews talked to Tevin for a while and urged him to stay away from people like Julius. Mr. Matthews told Tevin that he had known Julius for a long time and that he had been involved in a lot of bad things through the years. He said Julius had served time in prison and the only friends he had were criminals and they were always in some kind of trouble. Mr. Matthews asked Tevin if that was the kind of life he wanted. Tevin said this was not what he wanted.

This incident made Tevin think long and hard about what he was doing. He knew he could have been killed just that quick and he also knew even though Julius had been arrested, he was not going to just go away forever. Tevin remembered his conversation with Mr. Matthews but he also knew Julius would want revenge and the rest of his money. Tevin saw only one way to solve this problem and that was to get Julius' money any way he could and get this thing taken care of. Tevin was pretty confident that he had gotten away with stealing the money from his teacher. He knew he could do that kind of thing again and come up with the money he owed Julius.

Tevin knew he needed a large amount of money and stealing purses might not be the way to get it. He needed a bigger target. Tevin decided to rob a store. He did not have a gun so he would have to either get one or find a way to make the store clerk believe he had one. Tevin had a plan. He was sure it would work. No one would get hurt and he would get the money he needed to pay Julius back. He might get a lot of money and have some left over for himself. The more he thought about it the better it sounded. Tevin went home and began to put his plan into action. He decided he would rob the store down the street from his house. He would wait until closing time to go in. They knew his face in that store so he would have to wear a mask. Tevin thought about it all night. He was scared but he knew he had to make a move or Julius would surely kill him when he got out of jail.

The next day he got out one of his hats that covered his face. He had a black hoodie he was going to wear. Tevin had found a toy gun he had since he was a little kid and he would use it to scare the clerk. He was getting excited about all the money he was going to get. He could hardly wait for closing time for that store. They closed at 11:00 p.m. It was a school night and he would have to sneak out of the house after his mother had gone to bed. It was about 10:30 and Tevin put on his mask and hoodie and put the toy gun in his pocket and crawled out his bedroom window. It only took him a few minutes to walk to the store. He could see the clerk inside and there was one customer at the counter. Tevin waited until the customer drove off and he went into the store. When he came face to face with the clerk, Kevin was sweating and he was so nervous that he was unable to say anything to him. He knew what he was doing was wrong, but he needed the money. He was very confused in his mind about what to do. He had this whole thing all planned out and now he was frozen and could not make a move. He was scared and he quickly turned around and went out the door. His heart was pounding as he ran toward his house. He had gotten away with stealing the purse from his teacher and probably could have gotten away with robbing a store! Tevin decided to keep cool for a while and try it again another time.

Tevin's family members could see that Tevin was getting deeper into a lifestyle that was going to get worse if he did not change something. None of them really knew how deeply involved Tevin already was. His mom and his sister tried talking to him many times about the consequences of a life of drugs and crime but he would not listen. Tevin's dad, Gary, also tried to talk to Tevin about where he might end up if he continued on the road he was on. Tevin would not listen to his dad, either. Gary was concerned about his son.

Tevin's mother, Theresa, had been contacted by

Ms. Johnson, a school counselor, and asked if she could come in and talk with her. Theresa went to the school to speak with the counselor and find out what was going on. Ms. Johnson said that Tevin had always been a pretty good student and he was respectful to the teachers and other staff members. She said some of the teachers had voiced a concern about Tevin that he had been hanging out with some unsavory company and his behavior had changed, his grades were dropping and he seemed to show no interest in school anymore. It was suspected that he was dealing drugs in the school. Theresa admitted that she had seen a change in him as well, but she could not believe he was dealing drugs. She told Ms. Johnson that she just did not know what to do, she was a single mother and she worked as much as she could to support her children and their father was rarely around. Ms. Johnson said she understood and that she was a single parent herself and she knew how challenging it was to raise children alone.

Ms. Johnson told Theresa about a mentor program that was offered by the school for free. She said she had seen many children come into this program that were angry at the world and their lives were turned around by learning how to re-direct their way of thinking by going through this program.

Ms. Johnson assured Theresa there was help available and there were counselors on call ready to talk to Tevin any time he wanted to talk.

Theresa was upset about Tevin but she left the school with a sense of hope that she did not have before she talked with the counselor. She was determined to get Tevin into this mentor program. She just had to find a way to convince him it was the best thing to do. That night Theresa talked to Tevin and she also listened closely to what he had to say. Tevin expressed his anger about his dad not being there or helping them and how he hated seeing his mom struggle so much all the time about the bills. He told his mom he did not want to keep living that way. Tevin had finally let his guard down and was able to talk to his mom about how he really felt for the first time in his life. Theresa was finally listening to him. Theresa gently presented the mentor program to him and told him there were people there who had been through the same kind of things he was going through. She asked Tevin if he would be willing to go and check it out. Tevin reluctantly said he would.

Tevin went to his first meeting a few days later and he was surprised to find people who sincerely wanted to help him, people who really cared. Tevin had developed a belief that he could never trust anyone. After only a short time in the program he was able to change that belief. He saw first-hand that not everyone was only out for themselves. He learned that his anger was only hurting him and not helping anything. Eventually Tevin had completely distanced himself from the people he had previously been associated with and had developed friendships with people in his own school who were focused on the positive side of life and he liked having them as friends. Tevin's life was dramatically changed by what he learned through the mentor program.

Chapter 3

KEIRRA'S LIFE WITH GARY

Keirra and Gary were happy with each other when they first moved in together but it did not take long for things to start falling apart. Gary's hours were cut at work and it was difficult to pay child support on time. The financial strain began to take its toll. He was late paying most of the time and there were months when he did not pay at all. Theresa would call on a regular basis to ask Gary why he hadn't paid child support. Keirra could hear Theresa complaining about having lost her job and not being able to pay the bills. She told Gary she had gone to the Department of Family and Children

Services to get some help but she had to fill out all kinds of paperwork and they made her an appointment to come back in two weeks. Theresa told Gary she needed help now; she could not wait two weeks. Keirra tried to avoid answering the phone. She did not like being in the middle of all this. She felt bad for Theresa but there was nothing she could do. Gary was afraid that if he could not pay child support for a month or two that Theresa would report him and he would go to jail.

Keirra and Gary eventually had to move into a cheaper place because they could not pay the rent. Things seemed to only be getting worse. Keirra's dream of a wonderful life with Gary was not turning out the way she had hoped. She was still asking herself the same questions:" Why is my life so miserable? Why can't I be happy?"

After a few years with Gary, he began to withdraw from Keirra. He seemed to be gone a lot and Keirra felt alone. When he was there they argued a lot. She often felt abandoned. She was unhappy and she did not know how to fix it. It seemed to her that she had tried everything and nothing was working.

After spending most of her weekend alone,

Gary came home late Sunday night. He said he had spent the day with Tevin. Sometimes Keirra wondered if he was telling her the truth. She knew he had lied to her before and she did not know if she could trust him any longer. Gary went straight to bed and Monday morning after he went to work, Keirra considered leaving him. She had no job, no money, no transportation, no place to go. "How can I keep living like this?" she asked herself.

Her thoughts were racing back and forth about her life and how she had been treated over the years. She wondered why life had been so unfair to her. She felt like there was no way out. All her life she believed it was her fault that her parents were divorced. She really had no concrete reason but she was sure it was her fault and she lived in guilt. Keirra loved her dad so much but she believed she was a burden to him. Keirra was angry as she picked up a coffee cup and threw it against the wall. She could not control her emotions and she began to sob and cry out. As her tears were flowing she thought about killing herself. She wondered if anyone would really care. She spent the day focusing on the confusing and violent thoughts that were going through her head.

It was late in the afternoon when Keirra went to

the cabinet and found a bottle of wine. She drank it straight out of the bottle as she thought about all the empty promises Gary had made to her over the years. She was painfully aware that he was old enough to be her daddy and she was bewildered that she had been so vulnerable at sixteen to believe a man his age could be right for her. They had lived together for five years but most of that time, neither one of them was happy. Keirra concluded that Gary initially wanted her for a "play toy" and he really did not care about her at all. The more Keirra drank, the more convinced she was that suicide was the answer. Keirra found a bottle of prescription pain pills in the medicine cabinet. She emptied the bottle into her hand and began to swallow them until they were all gone. She was already so intoxicated from the wine she could hardly stand up. The pills took effect quickly and Keirra passed out on the floor.

It wasn't long before Gary came home from work and found her unconscious. He immediately threw her in the car and rushed her to the hospital. Fortunately, it had not been very long since she took the pills and they were able to pump her stomach before all the drugs got into her system.

The nurse came in to speak with Gary and asked him if he knew Keirra was pregnant. Gary looked shocked and said he did not know. Keirra was admitted overnight and when she was able to talk, the doctor came in and asked her if she knew she was pregnant. Keirra had suspected but she really did not know. She told the doctor she was not sure. The doctor then told her she was pregnant but they were not able to save the baby. Keirra broke into tears and Gary tried to comfort her. They both cried.

Keirra stayed overnight in the hospital and was released the next day. Gary stayed with her to make sure she was okay. While Keirra was waiting to be released, a counselor came in and she asked Gary if he would give them a little time alone. He went down to the lobby to wait. Keirra still felt sick and did not really want to talk. Anyway she did not think there was anyone who would understand what she was going through. The counselor gave Keirra the address and phone number of a clinic where she could get help. Keirra thanked the counselor and told her she would consider visiting the clinic. The counselor left and Keirra got dressed to go home.

Things were a bit awkward between Gary and Keirra after this incident. Gary really did not know what to say to her and she did not want to argue with him any more so they did not talk much when she first got home. When they did finally start talking they blamed each other for what had happened. Keirra thought going to the clinic for counseling would be a waste of time. Within a year after her attempted suicide, she and Gary split up. Keirra was severely depressed. She could not stop thinking about how Gary had treated her and she felt such guilt about losing the baby.

Chapter 4

A NEW BABY

Keirra stayed with friends or family off and on until she found a job and got a place of her own. Keirra worked hard and was finally able to support herself. She moved into a small apartment. She was just getting a new start in life when she met Shon. It was like love at first sight. Shon was cute and sweet. He had a great sense of humor and he made her laugh. Keirra had not laughed much in the last few years.

Keirra was a little hesitant to start a new relationship but it did not take long before she was deeply involved with Shon. They moved in together after a few months of dating. Keirra knew that Shon did not have a job and that he was a drug dealer. Keirra wanted to believe Shon was different from all the rest of the guys she had been with.

Shon kept his business transactions away from home in the beginning and Keirra really never knew what he was doing and she was okay with that. She really did not want to know, she just wanted Shon to love her.

After about a year together, Keirra became pregnant. She had some mixed feelings at first because of losing the first baby. She still had a deep sense of guilt because of what she had done. Eventually she was happy about having a child. Shon was excited too. They were planning their future and trying to decide on a name for the baby.

Shon soon became more involved in some illegal activities that required him to be gone a lot more. He was now dealing on a deeper level with some very shady characters. Keirra went through much of her pregnancy alone because of Shon's new business dealings. Keirra and Shon began to argue a lot and it often turned violent.

Kierra now had a beautiful baby girl named Davon. Davon was the love of her life and Keirra always wanted desperately for her baby to have a happy childhood. But this would not be the case. Keirra was suffering from post-partum depression. She struggled every day to enjoy her gift from God- her baby girl. Keirra loved Davon very much but she felt very much alone trying to make life work. Keirra had met Shon, who she thought was the "man of her dreams". They were married soon after they met and the happy life she experienced with Shon did not last long. She and Shon were together but Keirra always felt so alone. Shon was always gone and when he was there he was not supportive at all and Keirra had shed so many tears in a house that felt so empty. She felt her hope fading away and sometimes she just wanted to give up. Keirra did not want to continue to exist this way but she didn't really know what to do. She was so tired of the yelling and the fighting but it seemed to never end.

Chapter 5

THE LAST HAPPY CHRISTMAS DINNER

Shortly after Keirra's Mom and Dad had divorced, both of them were re-married. This was often very difficult for Keirra because there always seemed to be a lot of strife between her mom and her Dad's wife. Keirra was feeling very sad about her family being so separated, especially this time of year. She was once again remembering how it used to be when she was a child. She wanted so much to spend Christmas Day together with members of her family. She believed it would improve her spirit if the family could have Christmas dinner together again, despite their conflicts with one another. The division between her family was growing wider and wider and she thought this might be the last time they could get together like they used to. She felt that she had to try and make it happen. She could only hope everyone else would agree to come together.

"Well, here goes", she thought, as she hesitantly picked up the phone to call her mother, Gina. As the phone rang on the other end, her mind raced back and forth wondering how she would ask her mother and her husband, Jim, to come over. She almost hung up the phone thinking she would do it later when she had her speech prepared just the way she wanted it. But before she could hang up, she heard her mother's voice say, "Hello?" She fumbled in her mind for the right words. There seemed to be no other way than to just come right out and say what she wanted. "Mama, I want you and Jim to come over to my house for Christmas dinner. I planned on inviting Daddy and his wife, Rita. I want you all to get along this Christmas."

Gina replied, "Kierra, honey we will try to come over but only if you let me prepare Christmas dinner. I don't want Rita in your kitchen. I know she doesn't like me. I think she is jealous and she believes I still want to be with your daddy. It is difficult for me to be around her. I hope you can understand."

Keirra's heart sank when she heard these words. She said, "Mama, I don't want you and Ms. Rita arguing or trying to control everything. It is not a contest. I just want our family to be together and get along. Even though your grand- daughter is just a baby I know it would be good for her to spend Christmas together with you and Daddy there."

Her mom reluctantly agreed to come for Christmas and she said to Keirra," We will be there. I will try to get along with Rita. I don't know about how she will act. You know what I mean, you know how she is!"

Keirra held back the tears as she said good-bye to her mom. She wanted so much for this to be a pleasant time for everyone. Now she had to make another phone call. Davon was crying and hungry so Keirra fed her while she made the call. She was not sure this conversation would be any easier than the one she just had with her Mom.

Keirra was hoping her dad would be the one to answer the phone. It would be easier to talk to him. She liked Rita, she was nice, but she was still more comfortable speaking with her dad. Rita answered. Her dad was at work so she decided to ask Rita instead of calling back when her dad got home. "Good morning, Ms. Rita. I hope I'm not calling at a bad time, I have something I would like to ask you." Rita assured her she was not busy and that she had time to talk. Keirra said, "I would really like for you and Dad to come over to my house for Christmas dinner. My Mom and Jim will be there. My mom wants to prepare the meal. I know it will be a bit awkward for everyone but I want us all to be able to get along and spend time together as a family." Rita replied, "Kierra, I don't think your Mom likes me and I'm not sure this is a good idea. I must talk to your dad about it first" Keirra found herself pleading with Rita as she said, "This is very important to me. No matter what, I want you and Dad to be there. I understand that you and Mom have issues with each other but can't you just put those things aside so we can spend Christmas together?" Rita responded, "I hear what you are saying and I understand. Your dad and I will be there and I will try to get along with your mother." "You promise?" Keirra asked. Rita gently laughed and said, "Yes, I promise!" Keirra was so happy to hear that! As they said good-bye and hung up the phone, Keirra said excitedly, "We will have a great Christmas!" She was feeling much better already just knowing her mom and dad were going to be there.

It was about three weeks until Christmas and she could hardly wait. She had mixed emotions about the whole event. She was excited that the family was going to be together and she pictured everyone having a good time. But she was also afraid things might not go so well with her mom and Rita. She tried not to think about anything going wrong.

Keirra wished Shon would be more a part of the family. He seemed to not care very much what happened one way or the other. Keirra and Shon always struggled in their relationship. Shon seemed to be absent even when he was there and their arguing was getting more and more intense. The violence and anger seemed to be reaching a dangerous level.

Christmas day finally arrived and Keirra had cleaned up the apartment as good as she could and tried to get the kitchen in order for her mom to prepare dinner. She had managed to purchase a small Christmas tree and had just a few ornaments to decorate with. Everything was clean and festive. Her mom and Jim got there pretty early so she could start cooking. Her mom had already prepared some stuff at home the day before so it would not take so long to cook on Christmas day.

There was excitement in the air mixed with some anxiety. The delicious smelling fragrances of turkey and dressing, pumpkin pie, apples and cinnamon, and all the other yummy smelling food that came from the kitchen seemed to be enough to put anyone in a good mood. At least that is what Keirra hoped for.

Everyone finally arrived and after a few uncomfortable moments things began to lighten up a bit and everyone sat down to eat. It was wonderful to have her family together again for Christmas dinner. No one else said it, but Keirra thought they were all glad too, despite their differences. Even Shon seemed to be having a good time. Everyone talked and laughed while they had dinner. It was a moment Keirra wanted to hold onto forever.

Chapter 6

GIVING UP

The Christmas dinner with her family seemed to come and go in a flash. Keirra was hoping that everyone coming together that day would begin to heal some relationships in her family, but that did not happen. Everyone seemed to go right back to the same way they were before.

Davon was now a few months old and it seemed to Keirra that her life was just not going to change for the better. Even though she and Shon lived together she felt like a single parent. Keirra had to do everything for Davon by herself. Shon was never there to help out and when he was there he was mean and demanding. The atmosphere was usually pretty tense when Shon was at home.

Keirra's family was still pretty divided and everyone was distant. They all seemed to have their own lives and her Mom and Rita still were at odds with each other. Keirra knew she could never change that. She really missed spending time with her dad, but she had her own family now and things were so different. She thought a lot about how she would love to just be a kid again but she knew she could never go back there.   Keirra was very sad most of the time and she just didn't know how to change things. She asked herself, "How did I ever get in this place in my life?"

Keirra began thinking about all the stupid decisions that she had made in her life and realized that she had made her own life miserable by her own choices. She felt like she had messed up everything she ever did. She was so depressed and tired of trying to be happy and trying to make things work in her relationship with Shon. Her mind was in a place she could not seem to come out of. All of Keirra's thoughts were fighting to tell her she was no good and she had nothing to live for. Even when she thought about her baby, she thought Davon would be better off without her. Keirra did not think she could ever be a good mother to Davon and she might have a better chance growing up with someone else raising her. Keirra had thought about her first attempt at suicide many times. She was still so unhappy and depressed so she would try again to kill herself. She had a bottle of pills that she was sure would do the job. As she slowly opened the bottle, she was filled with fear and tears were streaming down her face. She was in so much pain and she just wanted it to stop. She did not know any other way to stop it so she started swallowing the pills until they were all gone. As Keirra began to feel numb all over, she slumped to the floor. She could not stand up. She was very dizzy and felt sick like she was going to throw up. She just wanted to hurry up and die. She wanted all the pain and suffering to end. It seemed like a long time that she lay on the floor almost unconscious. Keirra was unable to move. Suddenly there was a knock on the door. Keirra barely heard it, her ears were ringing so loud and she was just about to pass completely out. Her friend, Samantha, had come to see her. Samantha kept knocking and said, "Kierra, let me in. I know you are in there!" She finally opened the door and saw Keirra on the floor. Samantha ran to her and yelled, "Kierra! Wake up! Wake up!" Samantha called 911. An ambulance arrived shortly and took her to the hospital, where they were able to save her life.

When Keirra regained consciousness she was a little unsure of what had really happened. She knew she had tried to kill herself and she thought it was going to work for her. She could not really understand how she felt. She was disappointed that she did not die but at the same time she was glad someone cared enough to try to save her. She was very tired and confused. She was so ashamed of herself. Keirra did not know what her next step in life would be. She still felt trapped in a life of pain. She felt helpless.

Chapter 7

THINGS GET WORSE

The next few years were quite a challenge for Keirra. Things seemed to go from bad to worse. Keirra and Shon never seemed to have money and were living in government housing. It seemed like Shon spent most of the money he made and she was not really sure what it was spent on. Their apartment was extremely run down and needed a lot of repairs that never seemed to get done. They had very little furniture. What they did have was very old and broken down. They slept on a mattress on the floor and the couch had a broken leg so it had to be propped up with a board. Keirra tried to keep the place clean but there were still a lot of roaches. Davon was four years old now and she always wanted to go outside and play. Keirra had to keep a close eye on her because of the kind of neighborhood they were in. There was a lot of crime going on in this community. It was a very dangerous place.

Keirra would not dare let her go outside alone. She was still very cautious even when she was outside with Davon.

Month after month they struggled to pay the rent. It was paid late most of the time. Rent was due again in just about a week. Keirra and Shon were arguing about his plan to make money. He had made a connection with someone to obtain prescription drugs illegally so he could sell them on the street. Keirra thought this was a terrible idea but he insisted on doing it anyway. She knew Shon had been involved in buying and selling drugs for a long time. This was not really new to her but she just wished he would make money another way. This kind of lifestyle was putting all of them in danger. The people Shon had started dealing with seemed to be getting more and more dangerous. Keirra did not want Davon to grow up in this kind of environment.

Shon got up from the table and said he had to go take care of some business so they could pay the rent next week. Keirra knew she should not have said anything but she could not keep quiet. She said to him, "Shon, you are always in the streets, you never have time for me and Davon!" Shon angrily replied, "I am tired of you nagging me to stay here. You know I got to make some money so I can take care of things!" Keirra begged him to stay. "Shon, please wait until tomorrow. We need you to be with us." Shon yelled, "Get out of my face before I do something to you that I may regret later!" Keirra grabbed his hands and pleaded with him, "Please don't go!" Shon threw her on the floor and twisted her wrist until it broke. He walked out the door and yelled, "This is what you get for getting in my way! I am getting out of here now!"

Keirra started crying as she held Davon. Keirra wished Davon hadn't seen and heard all this. No child should have to experience this kind of violence and arguing and it was escalating. Shon was getting very angry so quickly about everything. Davon was scared and did not understand what was going on. Keirra tried to comfort her but she just kept crying and shaking with fear.

Keirra's wrist was aching and she was so angry and hurt. She also knew that on top of not having rent money she was going to have to find a way to pay to have her broken wrist taken care of.

All kinds of thoughts were now flooding into her mind. She was confused about how she had gotten so deep into this kind of life. Keirra loved Shon but she hated the way he treated her. She was so angry with him. Keirra believed they could be happy together if he would just stop being so meant to her. He just didn't seem to care at all. "Shon just keeps doing the same stuff that is destroying our relationship", she thought. Keirra didn't like the people he hung out with and she wished he didn't deal drugs. She would leave him if she could support herself and Davon. She didn't know what to do. Keirra just wanted Shon to love her. She felt like she and Davon were not important to him.

She could go live with her family. She just didn't want to. She felt like she would only be a burden to they and she would not have the freedom she wanted. Keirra knew her family members did not understand her and why she stayed with Shon. Anyway, Keirra believed she had caused her family enough pain.

Early in her Relationship with Shon, Keirra had indicated to her dad that Shon was becoming very aggressive when they argued but she did not tell him how severe things really were. Her dad knew it was worse than she was letting on. He was very concerned about Keirra and Davon. He told Keirra about a counseling service that dealt with domestic violence and urged her to get in touch with someone. Keirra had contacted a counselor a few times. They recommended that Keirra get away from him but she was so torn between being alone and staying in this situation she just did not know what to do. She believed Shon would change his ways. She considered calling her counselor but she was so distraught that she felt like it would be a waste of time.

CHAPTER 8

SHON'S NEAR DEATH ENCOUNTER

Later that evening Shon met with some of his buyers and they went to a local Pain Clinic where Shon was to get some pills they had ordered. Shon went inside while the others waited outside. He kept looking around to see if anyone was watching him. He waited patiently at the front desk. The receptionist asked if he had an appointment.   Shon told her he did not have an appointment but Dr. Wright knew he was coming in; he just needed to talk to him for a few minutes. The receptionist asked him what his name was and said she would tell the doctor he was here. Dr. Wright was with his last patient of the day and Shon had to wait a little while before he could see him. After about fifteen minutes or so the nurse called Shon into the doctor's office. Shon was very nervous just being in there and before the doctor could say anything Shon asked him if he had his package. Dr. Wright told Shon he did not have all of it and he would get the rest later on that week. Shon was a very agitated and almost yelled at the doctor, "I need it now, I got buyers waiting outside!" Dr. Wright tried to get Shon to calm down and told him to just tell them the truth. Shon had no choice but to go to his buyers without all the pills they expected. He was apprehensive about going outside because he knew they were waiting for him and he was not going to deliver. He was not sure how they would respond.

Shon walked out of the clinic with the bag of pills with his head hanging down. Before he could even get out of the door to the clinic, three of his buyers approached him to get their drugs. One of his buyers, Joe, asked, "Did you get my cut?" Shon replied, "I got some of it." Ricky, another dealer, said to Shon in a threatening manner, "You better have my cut now, Shon!" Patrick, the third buyer says, "I'm getting my cut now, I gave you money and I expect you to deliver!" Shon tells them the doctor did not have all of it and he would be getting it by the end of the week. They immediately accused him of lying. They thought he had taken part of their cut and told him he better come up with the pills now. Shon was afraid there was going to be trouble because he did not have all of the pills. They were angry because they had given Shon the money and he could not fill their order. They kept accusing him of stealing some of their pills. Shon tried to convince them he was telling the truth about what the doctor said and he could not get all the pills until later in the week. They warned him that he better be telling the truth and he better have what they ordered in a few days or he would be in trouble. Shon told them he would give them everything they paid for. They all left and Shon went home. Somehow he knew they did not believe him. He was afraid of what they might do.

Shon did not tell Kierra what had happened at the clinic. He was lying on the couch watching TV and Kierra was in the kitchen looking for something for him to eat when someone knocked on the door. Shon walked to the door and saw the three buyers standing there. He did not realize they had followed him home. Shon was afraid but he went outside. Patrick pulled out a gun and shot Shon in the stomach. Keirra heard the gunshots and ran outside calling Shon's name. She saw him lying on the ground bleeding. She knelt down and grabbed hold of him. Keirra was screaming and crying. She is terrified. She always knew this kind of thing could happen and now it has become a reality. Shon was taken to the hospital where he almost died. The surgeons worked quickly to save his life. He spent a couple of weeks in the hospital.

Chapter 9

KEIRRA LEARNS THE DRUG TRADE

During this time Keirra was trying hard to figure out how to make money. She was desperate. She knew a lot of money could be made dealing drugs and she was considering this idea. She hated the thought of doing it, but what else could she do? She could not make enough money at a minimum wage job. Maybe she could just do it long enough to get them on their feet again. If she made enough money she could buy some things she really wanted... like some new clothes and some stuff for the baby...It was starting to sound like a good idea. Keirra thought she might even be good at this kind of work. She knew they were going to lose their apartment if she didn't do something fast.

She presented the idea to Shon and he told her

she did not know what she was getting into. He got angry and told her she would probably screw it all up and they would both go to jail. She reminded him of how much they needed to make money right now and he still needed time to recover from his gunshot wound. Keirra was determined and she told Shon she could learn how it was done and she would be careful. He was not in any condition to fight with her, so he agreed to let her try it.

Keirra remembered the last time she was at the local nightclub, one of the girls she knew, Tameka, was talking to her about how she had been making money selling pain pills. So Keirra got in touch with Tameka and she was able to connect her with others who were in the business. Keirra was amazed at how many people were doing this. She caught on very quickly about what to do and what not to do and who she could trust and who she couldn't. Keirra realized right away that there were not many people she could trust in this business. She proceeded with caution and her business grew quickly. Before long, Keirra was bringing in enough money to pay all the bills. Keirra remembered how she had thought at first how she would only do this long enough to get them on their feet but making money selling drugs was so easy. She could never make this kind of money this quick by working at a regular job.

Keirra had become a bit cocky and controlling now that she was bringing in the money. She had her own car now and she was gone a lot. Keirra started liking hanging out at the club and she had money to go there not only for business but for fun. She and Tameka were going to the club several nights a week and Keirra would always come home very late. Shon felt like he was stuck at home because he was taking care of Davon while Keirra was out. He suspected she was doing more than just business while she was out. He did not like Keirra's attitude and now the tables were turned; she was gone all the time and he was at home. Shon was still recovering from his injury so he was not quite ready to get back into the swing of things and he was letting Keirra make the money for now, but he did not trust her.

One night Keirra and Tameka had gone to the club to do some business with the club owner and after they had made a couple of drug deals, they stayed and had a few drinks. Keirra was dancing and having a good time. She and Tameka had met a guy who invited them to come over and party with him and his friends. Keirra wanted to stay a while longer so she told Tameka she would meet her at his guy's house later. Keirra left the club around closing time and walked outside, where she was met by Shon. Davon was in the car. Shon yelled at her, "Get in this car right now!" Keirra yelled back, "I'm not going with you, I'm going to meet up with Tameka and I will be home later!" The screaming and yelling continued as Shon threatened Keirra and demanded that she get in the car. Keirra tried to get away from him but he pulled out a stun gun and as he shocked her, he said, "You're not going anywhere!" Davon was scared and she was screaming at her dad to leave her momma alone but neither one of her parents was listening to her. Shon pushed Keirra into the car next to Davon.

The next day Keirra felt strongly that she had to do something to get away from Shon. He left to go somewhere that morning and while he was gone, Keirra called her mother and ask her if she could take care of Davon for a while until she figured out what she was going to do. Her mother agreed to take Davon. Keirra then called Tameka and asked if she could take her to pick up her car where she had left it the night before. She also asked Tameka if she could stay with her for a few days until Shon calmed down. Tameka told Keirra she would help her get her car back and she could stay as long as she needed to. Keirra packed her bags and waited for Tameka to come get her. When Keirra picked up her car she immediately took Davon to her mother's house and then she went to Tameka's.

Keirra was making enough money to get her own place but she did not have a real job or any kind of credit to qualify to rent an apartment. Keirra had met a guy at the club one night that made fake I.D.s for people. She had gotten his phone number just in case she ever needed his services. After searching through her purse, she found his number. She proceeded to call and ask him if he could provide her with a check stub with her name on it and the name of a company so she could use it as proof of employment when she filled out an application to rent an apartment. He said that would be no problem and told her how much it would cost. Keirra told him she would pay and she needed it as soon as possible. She had it that same afternoon.

After a few days at Tameka's house, Keirra decided to go back to Shon to see if they could work things out. She drove home and Shon was there. She told Shon they could get a fresh start and she had money and a way for them to get a new apartment. Shon agreed and they proceeded to make plans to move.

Chapter 10

THE FATAL ACCIDENT

They moved into the new place and Keirra continued to deal drugs while Shon stayed at home. She was so caught up in this lifestyle that she would not consider doing anything else now. Keirra was still staying out late and Shon never knew where she was. He finally demanded that she be home by 8:00 p.m. every night. The fighting continued. Keirra now voiced her opinion that because she was making all the money she was free to go when and where she wanted to. Shon became very angry and he grabbed Keirra by the throat. She tried to break free and he hit her in the face with his fist and gave her a black eye. While they were struggling Shon grabbed her arm and re-injured her wrist where it had been broken before.

Keirra grabbed her keys and ran outside and jumped into her car. She started the car and took off. She could see Shon in her rearview mirror getting in his car. She tried to get away from him but he quickly caught up to her. Keirra was going faster and faster and Shon was right behind her. Keirra picked up her phone to call the police and before she can speak to anyone, she lost control of the car and crashed into a tree. Shon's car came to a screeching halt and he jumped out and ran toward Keirra. Her car was so mangled and he could not get the door open to get her out. He could not tell whether or not she was alive. The police and ambulance arrived and they worked quickly to get the door to open. Shon watched as they pulled Keirra's lifeless body from the wreckage. Keirra did not survive the accident. Shon regretted having chased her and he cried out loud. He was angry at her but he did not want her to die.

Keirra's mother, Gina, was notified first of her daughter's accident. When she learned that Keirra had died, she broke down and cried. She knew she had to call Keirra's dad right away and tell him. David had been on a business trip and he was driving home when he got the call from Gina. She was crying when he answered the phone. He knew something was terribly wrong. Gina told David that Keirra had been in a car wreck and she did not make it. David was in shock and he could hardly believe it. He began to scream and yelled, "No! It can't be true!" He was crying uncontrollably and could hardly see the road so he pulled over and stopped. Gina told him what had happened and they cried together on the phone. After they hung up, David was alone and he felt like he was losing his mind. This was too much for him. The pain was worse than anything he had ever experienced. He could not scream enough, he could not cry enough; he could not get any kind of relief from this agony he was in. He sat there for twenty or thirty minutes trying to decide what to do. He knew he had to do something. David started driving again. He knew he needed to talk to someone and the only person he could think of was the domestic violence counselor Keirra had talked to off and on for about three years. David had saved the number he had given to Keirra. He could hardly see the screen on his cell phone through the tears but he was able to contact Keirra's counselor, Fonda.

David was crying as he told Fonda about the phone call he had just received from his ex-wife about Keirra's accident. He told her he was driving home from Birmingham and he had about four more hours to travel and he just did not know who else to call. Fonda was very patient and understanding. She knew he needed help now. She gently suggested that he to pull over and stop so he could try to get himself together enough to drive safely. David told her he was going to keep driving; he did not think he could sit still. Fonda assured him they would get through this together, he would not be alone. She said she would stay on the phone with him as long as he needed her to, as she tried to calm him down so he could pay attention to the road.

Fonda tried to encourage David as she told him that Keirra had often talked to her about how much she loved him. She told him that Keirra always said he was her best friend and how she could tell him anything and he never judged or criticized her. Fonda told David that Keirra knew her daddy loved her and she loved him just as much.

David finally made it home and he was very grateful for the help he got from Fonda. He knew he might not have made it if she had not been there to see him through while he was travelling.

Chapter 11

SAYING GOOD-BYE

Everyone gathered at the River Waters Ministries to view the body of Keirra, a beautiful young woman, who had died way too soon.   There was quite a mixed crowd of people. Keirra's father and mother, her sister and her brothers were there. The church was full of Keirra's friends, some were drug dealers, and some of the girls were dressed like 'ladies of the night'. There were guys with the saggy pants on. Everyone seemed to be from a different kind of world, but that day they all had something in common, something very sad. They were all mourning the loss of Keirra. She had touched many lives and they were all there to say their last good-byes.

Pastor Scott was now at the podium and everyone was seated. He said, "Good afternoon! Today we are celebrating the homecoming of a young lady whose life was cut short due to a tragic accident. Keirra is only one of the many young people in this day and time whose life has been ended due to unfortunate occurrences. This is a very sad time for us all, but it can also be a time for us to realize we can make a difference in someone's life.

Keirra is no longer with us and only by the grace of God we are still here. We have the opportunity to make a difference in a young person's life today. Keirra had many struggles in her life. There are so many young people struggling with fear and doubt and anger and confusion. God did not create us to live a life of pain and suffering. He created us to love one another and support each other in times of trouble. Let us understand that God loves each and every one of us and knowing His love is what makes us happy and fulfills our lives. Remember, God loves you just like you are but He wants to help you live a life of peace and joy and freedom."

After the choir sings, Tameka goes to the podium to say a few words. She is crying and it takes her a minute to talk. She pulls herself together and begins." When it comes to describing who Keirra was and how great of a person she was, words will not even begin to give you an idea. She was a mother, a daughter, and most important to me, she was my friend. She felt like more of a sister to me. We always introduced ourselves to people as 'My sister from another mother!' We would literally go to war for each other. And just like sisters, we had our ups and downs. We would fuss but we were never to the point where we stopped being friends. I trusted

Keirra whole heartedly. And I knew she felt the same way toward me. There was a time in my life when I was going through so much. I was ready to give up because I felt like I could not take any more. I called her to talk and she encouraged me and told me everything would be okay. The words she used and the sincerity in her voice made it all seem better. Even before, when I was pregnant, I was really in a dark place and I wouldn't do very much. I just worked and went to school. I didn't want to hang out or talk to anybody. I cried most days. Keirra would come by almost every day to check on me. Some days I wouldn't even say anything to her. I would just lie in bed and she would come and lay down beside me. I don't know many people who would come and just sit and lay with you. That meant so much to me. People who knew her knew she was amazing. People who really didn't know her knew she was amazing. She would give you the shirt off her back. That's just who she was. I remember the first time I met her she talked to me like she had known me all my life. You don't meet people like that these days. Keirra made me feel comfortable just being around her. There were times when she showed signs that everything might not be okay, she still smiled and held it all together. Now looking back at those times, I remember seeing bruises and sometimes she would wear her hair covering her eyes because they were swelled. I wish I could have done something to help her."

Another one of Keirra's friends, Kelly, had some words to say about how much she loved Keirra and what good friends they were. She stated that she wished she could have been more help to Keirra during her times of trouble. Kelly expressed deep sorrow and apologized for letting her down.

Pastor Scott came back to the podium. He began by reminding everyone that trouble doesn't last forever. He quoted the scripture from Psalm 30:5. Weeping may endure for a night but joy comes in the morning. Pastor Scott said, "Keirra isn't here but her spirit will forever be in our hearts."

He tried to encouraged the congregation by letting them knows they had a choice in life and that they did not have to let people and circumstances overpower them and break them down. Pastor Scott said, "I know many of you have been trying to succeed in different areas of your life with no apparent progress. Do not give up! There is help for you! There is a deliverer who can deliver you from anything and set you free and His name is Jesus!" Almost everyone there was in tears as he shouted,

"Who wants to be free? We must stop making excuses and stop looking for answers outside of God's will. You may be going through a storm today but there is a way out. The Bible tells us in Psalm 23:4' Yea, though I walk through the valley of the shadow of death, I will fear no evil; for thou art with me; thy rod and thy staff they comfort me.' Somebody here today wants to be set free! There is no better way to celebrate Keirra's homecoming than to give you the opportunity to be free from your pain, free from your guilt, free from sin. This freedom comes from Jesus Christ. He is waiting right now for you to invite Him into your heart. If you want to be free, come forward now and allow Jesus to come into your life. There are counselors up here that will help you and pray with you."

Young people all over the church began to stand up and walk down the aisle toward the front of the church, including Shon. Many young people gave their life to Christ that day.

Chapter 12

THERE IS AN ANSWER

Many of you can probably relate to some of the characters and events that happened in this story, which is based on the lives of real people who had real experiences. Pain and suffering seemed to be the normal way of life for the families and individuals in this story. It was an everyday occurrence in their lives. You may feel the same way about your life. The question most people ask is, "Why?" Most of the time this question is never answered or the answer we get usually comes from someone who bases the answer on their own reasoning or who they tend to take sides with in a situation. There is an answer to why bad things happen to people and how any problem you may be dealing with can be resolved. If you really want to hear a solution, keep reading!

Every person on the face of the earth has a standard from which they operate their lives. We make every decision from the standard we choose. We choose where we live, what kind of job we have, what kind of mate we have, what kind of food we eat, how we raise our children, what we watch on TV, how we respond to other people, events or circumstances.

Let's get a full understanding of exactly what a standard is and how we choose our standard. The dictionary describes standard as : **(1) something established as a rule or basis of comparison in measuring quality, quantity, etc. (2) used as, conforming to, a rule, a model, etc. (3) generally accepted as reliable or authoritative (4) typical or ordinary**

The root word of standard is 'stand'. **To stand for something is to have a specific view or perspective. It is having a strong attitude or opinion about something. To stand is to take a position or make a declaration according to what you believe.**

We all live by a standard even if we don't realize it. Even people who seem to just 'go whichever way the wind blows' are living by a standard. Their standard may be that they are taking a strong stand to not put forth any effort to do much of anything. Their standard may be a belief that they just have to endure whatever comes along.

If our lives are in a mess then we can choose a different standard to live by. We have a perfect example of the perfect standard in the Bible. Jesus taught a certain standard. I am NOT talking about living your life according to the do's and don'ts of religious rules and regulations, even though that is a standard as well. Jesus Christ taught us about a standard of thinking. He showed us in His word that everything which happens in our life is a result of our way of thought. We all have a certain way of thinking and it stems from how we were raised and what we were taught as children. Many of us come from different backgrounds and our parents had different beliefs about how to raise children and our parents were all raised according to their parent's beliefs and traditions and it goes on and on back to our ancestors from as far back as possible. Now you might question how you could be affected by a great great great great uncle who died a hundred years or so before you were born. Even if we never knew any of our relatives we still are affected by their beliefs. They are passed down from generation to generation.

This poem speaks volumes about how children form their standards as they grow up. It was written by Dorothy Law Nolte in 1972.

"Children Learn What They Live"

If children live with criticism; they learn to condemn

If children live with hostility; they learn to fight

If children live with fear; they learn to be

apprehensive

If children live with pity; they learn to feel sorry for themselves

If children live with ridicule; they learn to be shy

If children live with jealousy; they learn to feel envy

If children live with shame; they learn to feel guilty

If children live with encouragement; they learn confidence

If children live with tolerance; they learn patience

If children live with praise; they learn appreciation

If children live with acceptance; they learn love

If children live with approval; they learn to like themselves

If children live with recognition; they learn it is good to have a goal

If children live with sharing; they learn generosity

If children live with honesty; they learn truthfulness

If children live with fairness; they learn justice

If children live with kindness and consideration; they learn respect

If children live with security; they learn to have faith in themselves and in those about them.

If children live with friendliness; they learn the world is a nice place in which to live

I have always loved that poem because it is so true. When we grow up in a negative and hateful environment then that is what we learn. Hatefulness becomes our standard. If we grow up in a loving environment then that is what we learn. Love becomes our standard. We form opinions and beliefs as children and typically carry those opinions and beliefs into our adulthood and then we teach them to our children and we expect them to be just like us. However, there is much more to it than just learning to be like our parents or whoever raised us.

During Jesus ministry here on this earth he taught only one thing and that was the Kingdom of Heaven. He made it very clear just what and where this kingdom is. Everyone thought this Kingdom he talked about would involve soldiers and weapons and powerful rulers. In Luke 17:20-21 when the Pharisees, the teachers of the law, asked him when this kingdom would appear, he answered them and said, "The kingdom of God comes not with observation...the kingdom of God is *within* you."

They did not understand and many people today do not understand. The kingdom of God is the power of God. We could re-phrase Jesus' statement by saying, "... the power of God is *within* you." The place within us where that power exists is in our mind. Our thought life is our power. It is our personal kingdom and we have the freedom to use this power however we choose. No one chooses for us unless we allow them to, and even then it is our choice.

Our standard of life comes from what we believe to be true. Our standard is the belief we have established to be what rules or governs all our decisions. We form a specific view or perspective about how things are and how things should be. Many people never even question whether or not another perspective could be valid. Most people just continue to take a stand for what they believe even if they do not have any kind of understanding as to why they believe the way they do. Where do our beliefs come from? Mostly from the way we were raised and as we get older we are strongly influenced by what we hear in churches or by what our grandma told us or from our friends or by politicians or many other loud voices in this world. Many different people say many different things but what are we to believe? There can be only one real truth and when we understand that truth, we are then free to exercise our power to benefit our lives and the lives of others.

It is easy to see that most of the characters in this story had a standard of life, a belief about life that led to misery and a life-long struggle. They all wanted to be happy and free, but each person had a way of thinking that would not allow happiness or freedom. It was not their circumstances or their parents or society that made them lives the kind of life they lived. It was their beliefs that caused them to make the choices they made.

Keirra was a wonderful person. She wanted a happy life and she worked very hard at all the things she thought would give her this life. Keirra was struggling with something we all tend to struggle with at some point in our lives. She lived with a sense of guilt and self-hatred. This guilt may have originated from the possibility that she may have felt it was her fault her parents got divorced. Many children from broken homes often feel this way, even though it is not their fault. Many children from broken homes or dysfunctional homes develop a belief that everything is their fault. This is not always a conscious belief but it is usually deeply embedded in a person's inner being. This kind of mind set creates a standard of life. This person will go on to see everything through the lenses of their belief about themselves. When someone has a sense of guilt within them they try to balance it with blame with comments and thoughts such as, "I may have done this wrong, but look how wrong you were!" It may be more subtle than that but they tend to look for wrong in another person. Romans 2:1 tells us, "...for wherein thou judgest another, thou condemnest thyself; for thou that judges doest the same things."

All these things; guilt, self-hatred, blame, forgiveness are mental states. We develop these by our patterns of thought. Keirra had developed a pattern of thought that led to her way of life. Even though she wanted to be happy, she believed her life was miserable all the time. Her continual train of thought was, "Why is my life so messed up?" or "Why do these same kinds of things keep happening to me?" She may have been asking some of the right questions but she was not getting the right answers. Her answers to herself were because she was a bad person because of things she had done, or because of other people in her life or her circumstances were the cause. She believed that her inside misery was caused from outside situations. This was not the truth. Keirra believed it was the truth, just as most people do. She saw herself as a victim of circumstance, that she could do nothing to change things, that she had no choices. She may have also believed she deserved to be punished. Keirra felt stuck in an atmosphere of hopelessness.

Keirra did have a choice. She chose to continue in her pattern of thinking. This is why she attempted suicide two times. She believed she could not be happy. Keirra was looking to be loved. She already had what she was looking for but she did not realize it. She was looking for love all her life and she believed she could get it from men but she never got the love she wanted. The love Keirra wanted was the love that God gives. God loved Keirra all her life no matter what she did just as He loves you and me. Keirra's thoughts would not allow her to forgive herself and she could not be free.

We keep ourselves in bondage by our thoughts and we set ourselves free by our thoughts. Some people believe they can't change the way they think, they have developed a standard of life based on their inability to change. There is some truth to that statement if we try to use our own power to change. That is why we must allow the power of God to change us. We do that by faith, by belief, by being willing to change our standard of thinking. First, we must be willing. We must not be afraid of change. We cannot hold on to our old way of thinking and expect new results. II Timothy 1:7 "For God hath not given us the spirit of fear but of power and of love and of a sound mind." We are spiritual beings and that is where our power lies, within us. We have the power of God on the inside of us. We have the love of God on the inside of us. We have a sound mind, a disciplined mind. We also have a free will to use this gift God has given us. We can continue in our old way of thinking or we can use God's power to let Him change our thought patterns. When we allow God to change us we will have the freedom and joy the Bible talks about.

There is one person in this story who did make a change at an early age and it probably saved him from a life of misery. His name was Tevin. Tevin was a very angry young man who felt hurt and neglected for most of his life. He developed a standard of thinking that told him life was hard, no one cares, there is no point in trying, breaking the law and hurting other people is okay because you have to do whatever you have to do to survive, etc. Tevin grew up hearing his mother bad mouth and complain about his father much of the time. She blamed Tevin's father for all that they were going through. It was his fault she got pregnant, his fault he left them, his fault they had no money, his fault that her life was so hard and on and on. This was their standard of thought. This was the normal acceptable way of thinking in his household. All their problems were someone else's fault and there was just nothing they could do about it.

When Tevin was offered the opportunity to go into the mentoring program he made a choice. He could have said "No" to the opportunity but something in him said, "Give it a chance". He could have continued to think the way he was raised to think and continue in the life of pain and suffering. But he made a positive choice that led to more positive choices that put him on a new path in life. Choosing to enter the mentoring program was only the beginning. He actually began to learn that he could choose to think differently. He did not have to focus on all the bad stuff that had happened in his life. He could find good and focus on that and when he did he began to see things change for the better. Good things became a reality. He did not have to live with the same standard or beliefs he had grown up with. He had the power to change his thoughts and he developed a new standard that was based on knowing the truth about how his thoughts directly affected his life. Just because his mother believed his father was a bad person and this is what she focused on and talked about and this is how she experienced him and everything else in her life, did not mean Tevin had to continue to think this way. Tevin's mother really struggled because she believed struggling was the way of life.

The kingdom represents power and authority. We have the power of God within us. The Bible tells us in John 4:24 that God is a spirit. Genesis 1:25 tells us we were created in the image of God. We are not just flesh and blood, we are spiritual beings and we are creators. We create within our thoughts. Nothing has ever come into being that wasn't first a thought. Our thoughts create our reality. Our kingdom is our thought life. We first form a thought and if we focus on that thought long enough it begins to manifest in our physical world. It does not matter if the thought is a positive one or a negative one.

Most people take on the same standard, or way of thinking, as their parents because that is what they learned growing up. Most of us do not consider changing our standard of thinking. We think about changing outside standards, like driving a better car or wearing the latest fashions or living in a better house and those kinds of things. Even if we work real hard all our life and are able to change some of those things it does not change the person on the inside.

We do not have to continue to think or believe the same way our parents or our grandparents did if it is not benefiting our lives or the lives of others. Changing our way of thinking is kind of like working out with weights. It takes some effort to get results. If we are not used to it, even lifting a five or ten pound weight several times is a challenge. Afterwards our muscles are sore but if we continue to do it, the soreness goes away and we begin to lift heavier weights, and we are more confident and it does become easier. The weights are still heavy but we now believe we can do it and the fear of lifting a heavy weight is gone. The weights are always going to be heavy but if we continue to lift them we make progress. But we have to keep doing it or we will begin to lose that muscle tone we have built up.

Changing our way of thinking is the same thing. We have all developed habits of thought. There are some people who just can't seem to find any good in anything. For example, if you are excited about a new idea you have and you share it with them, they will always point out what is wrong with it or what could be wrong with it or tell you it is too costly or somebody else has already done that or whatever they can think of that is negative about your idea. This kind of person is always saying things like, "I would like to have a yard sale but it will probably rain all day." or "I'm sure when I get to the store I won't be able to find a parking place close to the entrance." or "I hope those people don't come visit me, my house needs to be painted and the grass needs to be mowed." Do you know anyone like that? I do! These kinds of people always expect the worst and they usually get it. These people are usually miserable and depressed on some level. But then there is the other side of the coin. The ones who have positive habits of thought. Even if you are having a tough time with something in your life, these are the people who will find something good in it no matter what the circumstances are. They will encourage you and lift you up. Their positive habits of thought keep them in a positive state of mind or spirit.

Both kinds of people have made a choice as to how they want to think about life. _Proverbs 23:7 As a man thinks in his heart_ (his mind) _so is he_ (so is his attitude and spirit which results in his circumstances). The results of our choice are always very clear. The Bible teaches us how we ought to think so that we get good results.

_Romans 12:2 Do not be comformed to this world _(this world's way of thinking) _but be **transformed** by the renewing of your mind..._

> •We can make a choice to change our habits of thought from hate to love. This transforms us. Always search for what is good in a person or a circumstance.

1 Corinthians 13: 4-8 Love suffers long, and is kind. Love does not envy, love does not parade itself, it is not puffed up, does not behave rudely, does not seek its own, is not provoked, **thinks no evil**, does not rejoice in iniquity, but rejoices in the truth, bears all things, believes all things, hopes all things, endures all things. Love never fails...

> •When we think in love we are in a positive state of mind. We become patient and kind and considerate of others. We are meek and not proud and arrogant. We are not easily angered or irritated. We think the best and not the worst. Love never fails and love is a deliberate choice. It is a mental state that we choose to be in.

•How we think and what we think about is the answer to how are lives are in reality. We have been given power to make choices. If you feel like your life is in pieces, do not be afraid to step up and make a new choice for yourself in changing your habit of thought. There will always be people who will come against you and try to keep you in a negative thought pattern. You do not have to stay there. It is your choice. Whenever you have a negative thought, remind yourself of these scriptures and choose a positive thought. You can begin a new way of life by a new pattern of thought right now. Do not delay and do not give up. Just like lifting weights, if you stick with it you will see results!

Founder of TSO Network Youth Theatre Church, Founder of Teens Speaking Out Radio Show and Performing Art Theatre Group, Founder of No More Pain Radio Show, Founder of the North East Mississippi Performing Arts Playhouse, Founder of Operation Hope Educational and Developmental Corporation, Pastor, Motivational Speaker, Counsellor, Life Coach, Teacher and Mentor. He lives in Albany, Georgia, with his wife.

David Hatch is the writer of the books, "Teens Speaking Out Are You Listening?", "The Twenty Commandments For Parenting A Child With ADHD", writer of the gospel musical plays: "The Will To Survive, I've Got It!" – based on his homeless episode and the people he met while homeless; "I Gotta Make A Change", "What About The Children Now?", and "A March Toward The Promise Land". Also writer of the scene play: "Pieces".

David has a Ph.D. in Christian Psychology, Master in Theology, and B.A. in Biblical Studies from Jacksonville Theological Seminary, three years in Business Administration, Mississippi Valley State University and two years in Computer Science, Waubonsee College.

"Pieces" is of utmost important to David because of the death of his daughter who died in a car crash after being chase by her boyfriend. This incident change David world and his view on life. Pieces described how domestic violence and abuse directly affected his family. This personal experience talked him how to forgive and let go of the pain inside.